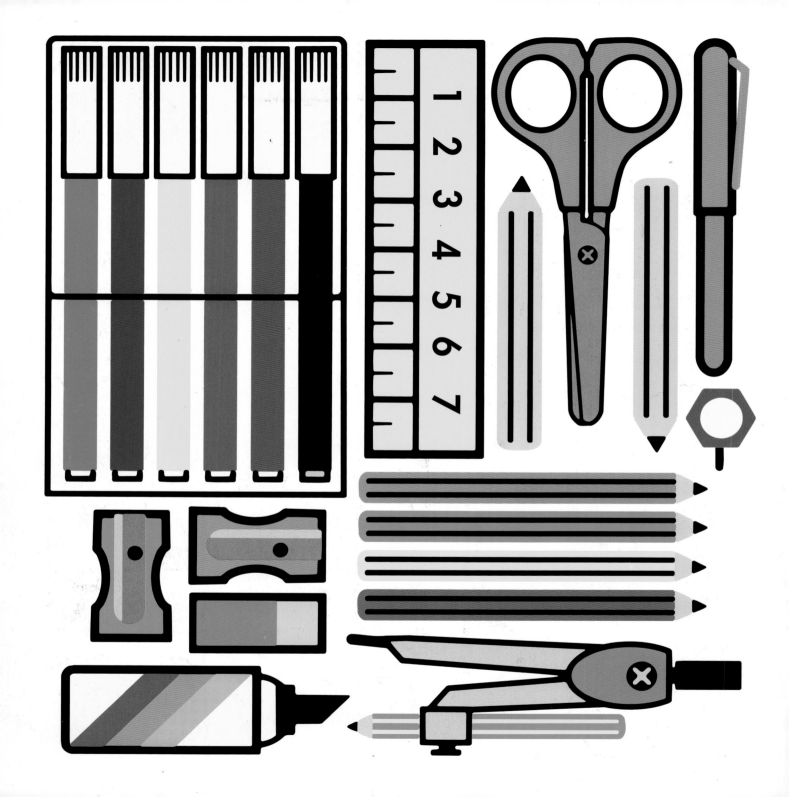

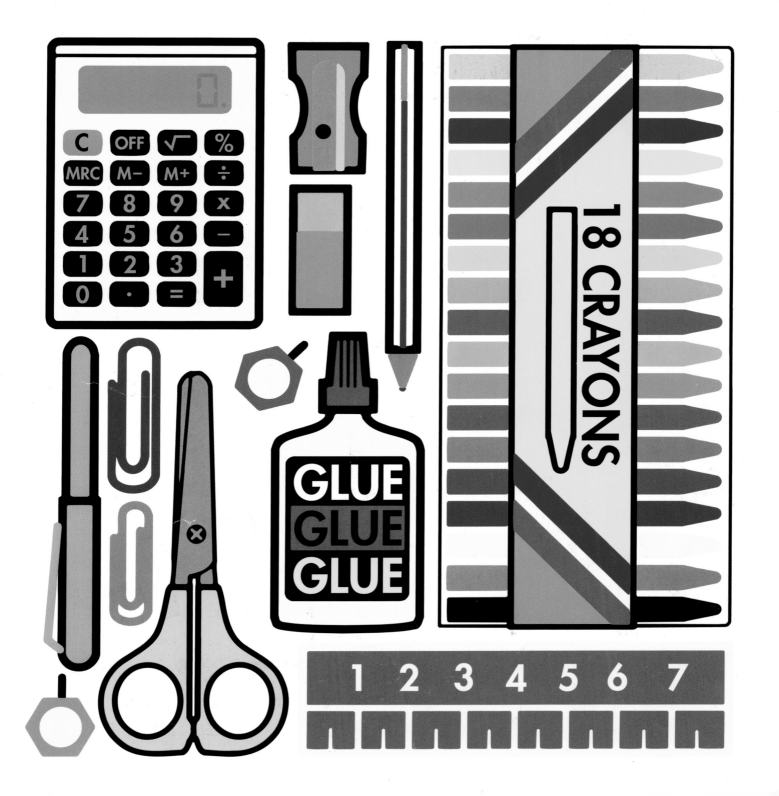

JONATHAN CAPE

UK | USA | Canada | Ireland | Australia
India | New Zealand | South Africa

Jonathan Cape is part of the Penguin Random House group of companies
whose addresses can be found at global.penguinrandomhouse.com.

www.penguin.co.uk   www.puffin.co.uk   www.ladybird.co.uk

Penguin
Random House
UK

First published 2018
001

Printed in China
A CIP catalogue record for this book is available from the British Library

ISBN: 978-1-780-08055-0

All correspondence to:
Jonathan Cape, Penguin Random House Children's
80 Strand, London WC2R 0RL

williambee

Stanley's
School

JONATHAN CAPE • LONDON

It's going to be another busy day at Stanley's school.

Hattie rings the bell. Ding! Ding! Ding!
Time for school!

The children hang up their hats,
bags and teddy bears.

Stanley ticks off the children's names in the register: Little Woo, Sophie and Benjamin. All here!

Stanley reads the children a story - it's all about a dragon, a knight and a princess.

Sophie dresses up as the dragon,
Little Woo dresses up as the knight,
and Benjamin dresses up as the princess.

After story time – it's playtime! Little Woo, Sophie and Benjamin act out the story that Stanley has just read them.

But Benjamin has made up a new ending . . .
RARRRR!

Stanley, Little Woo, Benjamin and Sophie are all in the school's garden. They have come to measure their sunflowers.

Benjamin and Sophie have watered their sunflowers every day - don't they look big? But Little Woo forgot to water his.

After all that storytelling, measuring and chasing about, it's time for lunch!

There is cheese and tomato pie for everyone, Stanley has made some lemonade, and Hattie has made a lovely fruit salad.

After lunch, everyone
has a little rest.

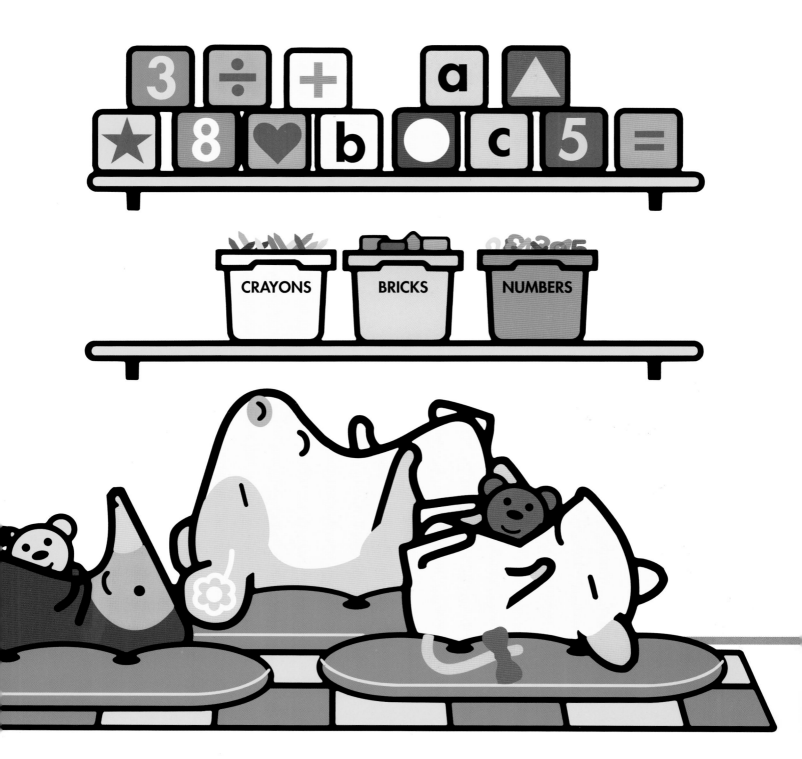

Little Woo, Sophie and Benjamin love painting!
Some of the paint ends up on the paper . . .

and the rest ends up on the floor,
the tables, and on Stanley and Hattie.

Hattie rings the bell. Ding! Ding! Ding!
It's home time!

Thank you, Stanley!
Thank you, Hattie!

Well! What a busy day!

by little woo

Time for tea!
Time for a bath!

And time for bed!
Goodnight, Stanley.

Stanley

If you liked **Stanley's School** then you'll love these other books about Stanley:

Stanley the Builder
Stanley's Café
Stanley the Farmer
Stanley's Garage
Stanley's Shop
Stanley's Numbers
Stanley's Opposites
Stanley's Colours
Stanley's Shapes

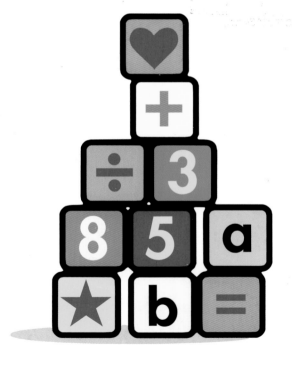